PENGUIN BOOKS

BITTER HERBS

Marga Minco was born in 1920 in Breda, a Catholic city in the south of the Netherlands. In 1938 she became a journalist, working for *De Bredasche Courant* until shortly after the German invasion in May 1940. Soon afterwards she entered a hospital, and later a sanatorium, for a long, much-needed rest that spared her from more calamitous events. After the war she married and resumed her career as a journalist.

Marga Minco's autobiographical stories and novels show her rejection of her Orthodox Jewish upbringing and reveal how she came to grips with the troublesome events of her childhood during the Second World War. It was during the period 1953 to 1955 that she first wrote a series of short autobiographical pieces for the Dutch periodical *Mandril*, and in 1957 her first novel, *Het Bittere Kruid (Bitter Herbs)*, appeared. It was a huge success in Holland and won her the Vijverberg Prize from the Jan Campert Foundation. She has since published two collections of stories, a children's book and three novels.

She now lives in Amsterdam, and her books have been published in Danish, English, French, German, Norwegian, Swedish and Welsh.

BITTER HERBS
A LITTLE CHRONICLE

MARGA MINCO

TRANSLATED FROM THE
DUTCH BY ROY EDWARDS

*Through my head rolls a train full of Jews; I switch
the past away like railway points* . . . – Bert Voeten

PENGUIN BOOKS

PENGUIN BOOKS

Published by the Penguin Group
Penguin Books Ltd, 27 Wrights Lane, London W8 5TZ, England
Penguin Books USA Inc., 375 Hudson Street, New York, New York 10014, USA
Penguin Books Australia Ltd, Ringwood, Victoria, Australia
Penguin Books Canada Ltd, 2801 John Street, Markham, Ontario, Canada L3R 1B4
Penguin Books (NZ) Ltd, 182–190 Wairau Road, Auckland 10, New Zealand

Penguin Books Ltd, Registered Offices: Harmondsworth, Middlesex, England

First published in the Netherlands as *Het Bittere Kruid*
by D. A. Daamen's Uitgeversmaatschappij. N.V.
This translation first published by Oxford University Press 1960
Published in Penguin Books 1991
1 3 5 7 9 10 8 6 4 2

Original illustrations by Herman Dijkstra

Printed in England by Clays Ltd, St Ives plc

CONTENTS

One Day

It began one day when my father said: 'We'll just go and see whether everyone's back.'

We had been away for a few days. The whole of Breda had been evacuated. In great haste we had packed a suitcase and taken our place in the endless lines of people leaving the town in the direction of the Belgian frontier. Betty and Dave, my brother and sister, were in Amsterdam at the time. '*They* won't know a thing about it,' my mother said.

It was a long, hazardous journey. We carried the case on a bicycle. Bulging bags hung from the handlebars. Bomb splinters and machine-gun bullets flew over our heads. Sometimes somebody got hit; when that happened a little group remained behind.

Close to the frontier we found accommodation with farm people. Only a couple of days later we saw the German occupation troops driving along the country road, and a few hours afterwards the evacuees started to return to the town. 'The danger's past,' a fellow-townsman came to tell us; and we went back with the rest.

At home, everything was just as we had left it. The table was still laid. Only the clock had stopped. My mother immediately threw open all the windows. On the other side of the street a woman was hanging her blankets out over the balcony to air. Somewhere else, someone was beating carpets as if nothing had happened.

I went up the road with my father. Our next-door neighbour was standing in his front garden. He walked down to the gate when he saw Father coming.

'Have you seen 'em?' he asked. 'No joke, what?'

'No,' my father replied. 'I haven't seen anything yet. We're going to have a look.'

'The town's swarming with 'em,' said our neighbour.

'I'm not surprised,' said my father. 'Breda's a garrison town—it's only to be expected.'

'I'm curious to know how long they'll hold out here.'

'Not long, I bet,' said my father.

"And what about you people?' the neighbour asked. He came closer. 'What are *you* going to do?'

'Us?' said my father. 'We're not going to do anything. Why should we?'

Our neighbour shrugged his shoulders and plucked a leaf from his hedge. 'When you hear what they've been up to over there. . . .'

'It won't come to that in Holland,' said my father. We went on our way. At the end of the street we met Mr. Van Dam.

'Well, well,' said he, 'look who's here. So we're all back home again.'

'As you see,' said my father. 'All back home again, alive and kicking. Seen many more of the old familiar faces yet?'

'Sure I have,' said Mr. Van Dam, 'several. The Meyer

boy's apparently gone on to the French frontier with some of his pals.'

'Oh well,' my father said, 'lads like that seek adventure. I can't say I blame them.'

'Your other daughter and your son didn't go with you, did they?'

'No, they're still in Amsterdam. They're safe enough there.'

'For the time being.'

'We'll be getting along,' said Father.

'What did Mr. Van Dam mean by "for the time being"?' I asked him as we walked on.

'He's rather pessimistic about things, I think.'

'Just like the man next door,' I said.

My father frowned. 'One can't tell yet,' he said. 'We'll just have to wait and see.'

'Do you think——' I asked, 'do you think they'll do the same to us as they've been doing to——' I didn't finish. I was thinking of all the horrible stories I had heard in the last few years. Until that day it had always been so far off.

'Things like that can't happen here,' said my father. 'Things are different here.'

The air of the little office of Mr. Cohen's dress shop in Catharinastraat was heavy with tobacco smoke. Several members of the Breda synagogue had come together there, as if for a parish meeting. Little Mr. Van Buren was swivelling to and fro in his office chair, gesticulating violently. He had a harsh, grating voice. As we came in he was talking about a special service to be held in the synagogue.

'I'm all for that,' said my father.

'Will that praying do any good?' asked Mr. Cohen's son. Nobody seemed to have heard, for nobody answered him.

I began to wish I hadn't come with Father. I realized that he wouldn't be able to leave here so quickly. As I didn't feel at all keen on sitting down and staying in that smoky room, I went out into the passage, to the shop.

There was no one there.

I walked past the counters and the racks full of articles of clothing. I had often played there as a child with the Cohen children. We hid behind the coats and boxes. We dolled ourselves up with ribbons and remnants of material from the workroom, and we played at keeping shop when the place was closed. The same smell still hung in the air, sweetish and dry, the smell new clothes always have.

I wandered through the narrow corridors to the workroom and the stores. It seemed like Sunday. No one would come to buy anything, or to be measured for a new coat, to-day.

I sat down to wait on a pile of boxes in a corner of the workroom. It was rather dark there, because the shutters on the outside of the window were closed, and the only light was what came in from the passage.

A lady's coat was hanging against the wall. The tacking threads were still in it. Perhaps no one would come to collect it now, I thought. I took it off the hanger and put it on. I looked at myself in the mirror. The coat was far too long.

'What on earth are you doing?' It was Father's voice.

I jumped. I had not heard him coming.

'I was trying on a coat,' I said.

'This is no time to be thinking about a new coat.'

'I don't want it, anyway,' I said.

'I've been looking everywhere for you. Are you coming?'

I took the coat off and hung it back on the hanger. Once outside, I noticed that I had been sitting in the dark a long time. I had to get used to the glaring sunlight.

The streets were busy. Many strange cars and motorcycles drove past. A German soldier asked someone walking in front of us the way to the market square. He was told, with much waving of hand and arm. The soldier clicked his heels, saluted, and walked in the direction he had been shown.

Soldiers of the occupying forces were passing us constantly now. We simply walked past them, quite normally.

'You see?' my father said, when we were almost home again. 'They won't do anything to us.' And as we walked past our neighbour's garden gate he muttered again: 'They won't do anything to us.'

Kloosterlaan

As children, my elder sister and I were sometimes called names by the other children when we came out of school. Often they would lie in wait for us at the end of the avenue called Kloosterlaan. 'Come on', Betty would then say, firmly, seizing me by the hand. Once or twice I timidly suggested we should take another road, or turn back. But she would stride on, dragging me along with her, straight towards the jeering mob. Lashing out to left and right of her with her satchel, she carved a path for us through the swarm of children, who punched and pushed us from all sides.

I frequently asked myself why we were different.

'Our teacher says Jews are bad people,' a neighbour's child once said to me. He went to a Catholic school. 'You murdered Jesus.' At that time I didn't yet know who Jesus was.

Once I saw my brother fight a boy who would not stop calling 'Dirty Jew!' after him. He only held his tongue when Dave had knocked him flat. Dave came into the house bleeding from a cut on the head. Whereupon Father showed us an old scar on his own temple, where a boy had gone for him with an iron nail, in *his* schooldays. '*We* got a lot of dirty words in Gelderland too,' he said.

I had a friend who regularly called for me, to go to school. Her name was Nelly and she had very fair hair. She always stayed outside our front door. She never came inside. When the door was open she peeped inquisitively into the hall.

'What does it look like, in your house?' she asked one day.

'Come in and see,' I invited her.

But she dared not, because her mother had forbidden her to go into houses where Jews lived. By then I had already reached an age when I could not help laughing at such things. I was eleven. I said that my father ate all children up, and that my mother boiled them down for soup first. After that she visited our house on the sly, without her mother knowing it.

When we grew older, we hardly noticed any of this any more. Children below the age of ten are often crueller than grown-ups. I do remember that we had a Catholic housemaid who had to ask the priest's permission before coming to work for us. The priest approved; he even told her she did not have to eat fish on Friday. That was a stroke of luck for her, for on the evening before the Sabbath we ate a very elaborate dinner, and all sorts of meat dishes were served at table.

My father was a religious man, who set great store by having a household in which the Jewish laws and ritual customs were observed. It must have been painful for him to see how we disregarded them more and more as a result of going about with Gentile friends, and in order to be able to take part in everything. It was most difficult for Dave. He was the eldest of us three, and he had to break all the laws first. He paved the way for his younger sisters. I still remember how I ate a fried leg of rabbit for the first time, with a friend, in a self-service cafeteria. I was doing something that was strictly forbidden. Before setting my teeth in the meat I hesitated, just as you do when you stand on the edge of the swimming-bath for the first time in the season. But if you persevere, even the second time is less difficult than the first; and so on.

During the Occupation the word 'forbidden' acquired another meaning for us. Jews were forbidden to enter cafés and restaurants, theatres and cinemas, swimming-baths and parks; they were forbidden to have a bicycle, a telephone, a radio.

So much became forbidden.

If I had still been a little girl, I should certainly have asked myself whether all this *was* because we had murdered Jesus.

In the first year of the war I fell ill. I had to go into hospital for treatment at the time when my parents moved from Breda to Amersfoort, to live with my brother, who had got married in the meanwhile.

I lay in the isolation ward of a hospital in Utrecht, and I was forbidden to leave my bed. For me, the progress of the war gave place to the progress of my blood sedimentation rate. The only distinction the doctors and nurses made as regards us patients was between serious and less serious degrees of t.b. Perhaps that was why I did not find the treatment so bad as I should have done if I had had to undergo it in normal times. Only during

visiting hours did the war and the new regulations come and sit beside my bed. But it was as if none of it applied to me—as if it all concerned another world.

When my condition improved I could no longer avoid it. I knew that, for me, to leave hospital was to step straight into the middle of Kloosterlaan—that the crowd of jeering children would be standing waiting for me, and I should have to struggle through it again.

The Stars

FROM the window of my bedroom I saw my father approaching in the distance. I had been out of hospital for some weeks. I still had to rest for a couple of hours each day, but I was quite well again.

The road in which we lived was all I knew of Amersfoort as yet. It was in a quiet suburb of new semi-detached houses, set in gardens. My father was walking along with short, firm steps, and raised his hat with a flourish to a woman who was standing in her front garden picking flowers. She appeared to say something to him, for he checked his pace for a moment. When he was close to the house I saw that he was carrying a parcel in his hand. A small brown parcel.

I went downstairs, stuck my head round the door of the sitting room, and announced:

'Here comes Father, with a parcel.'

I went towards the front door. 'What's in it?' I asked.

'In what?' asked my father, placidly hanging up his hat and coat. He had put the parcel on top of the hall-stand.

'What a question!' I said impatiently. 'In that parcel you've got there?'

'You'll see,' he said. 'Come.'

I followed him inside. He put it down on the table, while everyone looked curiously on. It was tied up with string, the knots in which he first patiently unpicked. Then he unfolded the brown paper.

It was the stars.

'I've brought several for each of us,' he said. 'Then you'll be able to sew them on all your coats.'

My mother took one from the parcel and examined it closely. 'I'll just see whether I've got any yellow silk in the house,' she said.

'They're orange,' I said. 'You'll have to use orange thread for them.'

'I think it would be better to take thread of the same colour as the coat you sew it on,' said Lottie, my brother Dave's wife.

'It'll look awful on my red jacket,' said Betty. She had come from Amsterdam to stay with us for a few days.

'I leave it to you,' my father said. 'But don't forget, they've got to be on the left side, at the height of your chest.'

'How do you know that?' asked my mother.

'It was in the newspaper, wasn't it?' said my father. 'Didn't you read it? They've got to be clearly visible.'

'What a lot you've brought,' said my mother, doling out two or three stars to each of us. 'Could you have as many as all that?'

'Oh, yes,' said my father, 'as many as I liked.'

'It's certainly convenient,' she said. 'Now we can keep some in reserve for our summer clothes.'

We fetched our coats from the hallstand and got down

to sewing stars on them. My sister Betty did it very carefully, with small, invisible stitches. 'You must hem them,'
she said, when she saw how I was fixing the star on my
coat with big, untidy stitches. 'That looks much neater.'

'I think they're such awkward things to sew on,' I
complained. 'How on earth can you get a hem round
those beastly points?'

'You have to turn the hem in first,' said Betty. 'Then
you tack the star on to your coat, sew it firmly in place,
and pull the tacking-thread out; if you do that, it's bound
to look all right.'

I tried again. I wasn't so skilful with needle and
thread as my sister. After all my efforts, the star was still
crooked.

'Now you can't read what's on it,' I sighed. 'But I
don't suppose that'll matter. They'll know all the same.'

'Look,' said Lottie, 'it fits exactly into one of the
squares on my coat.' We looked at her coat, which she
put on at once.

'*Very* nice,' my mother pronounced. 'You've done it
very neatly.'

Betty threw her coat on too. Together they walked
up and down the room.

'Good as the Queen's Birthday,' I said. 'Wait a moment and I'll put mine on as well.'

'Yours'll fall off in no time,' said Lottie.

'Oh no,' I said. 'It'll never come off.'

'What are you doing?' asked Dave. He had appeared
in the doorway, and was looking at us in surprise.

'We're sewing the stars on,' said Lottie.

'I'm looking for my overcoat. Has anybody seen it?' he asked.

'It's here,' said Lottie. 'It isn't ready yet.'

'I've got to go out,' said Dave. 'Can I still put it on as it is?'

'To-day you can still put it on as it is,' my father said.

'Would you like to wait a minute while I fix it for you?' I offered. 'I'm very good at it.'

'No,' said Dave, 'if I can, I'd like to be ordinary, for to-day.'

When he opened the garden gate and walked down the road, the five of us gaped after him as if there was something very extraordinary about him.

The Bottle

DAVE closely scrutinized the medicine bottle he was holding in his hand. It was filled with a brownish liquid.

'Are you ill?' I asked.

'No,' he said. 'What makes you think so?'

'That's medicine you've got there, isn't it?'

'That's for to-morrow,' he answered.

'For . . . er—nerves?'

'No, for something else,' he said.

'Is it dangerous?' asked Lottie.

'Maybe,' he said. He took the cork out and sniffed at it.

'Do you think you ought to do it, then?' said Lottie.

Dave shrugged his shoulders. He put the little bottle in his pocket and walked through the open french windows into the garden.

He picked up a stone from the gravel path and chucked it over the fence. I followed him out because my deck chair was ready, under the awning. I was still not allowed to lie right in the sun. Only my legs. I moved the chair so that the sun fell on its foot.

'What a long time it's lasted, hasn't it?' I said to Dave, who was standing with his back to me looking into the garden.

'What's lasted a long time?' he asked.

'My illness,' I said. 'I'm fed up with this everlasting lying down.'

'Think yourself lucky you're better,' he said.

'Does it make you ill?' I asked.

'Does what make you ill?'

'That . . . bottle.'

He shrugged his shoulders. 'It makes you feel a bit sick,' he said, 'but it's supposed to.' He turned and went back into the house.

The following day, Father and Dave, like all the other Jewish men in Amersfoort, were to be medically examined for the labour camps. Father did not think he would be accepted. He suffered from a chronic skin affection, which pleased him no end now. 'They won't fancy me, you see,' he said. I suspected he was doing something to make it worse.

I knew that Dave was also trying to think up a way of keeping out of the labour camp. As soon as the news was known he started to call on people he knew, and a few days later he said he had hit on something. At first I did not understand what the medicine bottle could have to do with it. I always associated medicine with getting better.

From the room behind me came the sound of a violin. It was a long time since I had heard my brother play. I twisted round in my chair and peered in through the french windows.

He was standing in the middle of the room, improvising a czardas. Lottie sat looking at him. His head was bent slightly forward, his hair falling over his face. I saw the fingers of his left hand moving over the strings. I turned and lay down again, to listen to his playing at my ease; but suddenly he broke off, and a moment later I heard the lid of the violin case slam shut.

Next morning I saw that little bottle in the bathroom. Cautiously I uncorked it. It smelt bitter. And now I perceived that some of its contents were gone already. It was just an ordinary small bottle, of the sort you see in every medicine cupboard. Only there was no label on it.

In the afternoon it was still in the same place, but it was empty and the cork lay beside it.

Just as I was about to go downstairs my brother came up. On the top stair he turned round and went back, after which he immediately came up again. He looked white, and drops of sweat stood out on his face.

'Does it work quickly?' I asked.

'Yes,' he muttered, ascending the stairs again.

'Is it really necessary to run up and down the stairs so often then, as well?'

'Everything's necessary,' he said. He paused for a second at the top, then ran quickly down. 'Going down's still easy enough,' he said, 'but I already have quite a job to get up again.'

'How long are you going on doing that?' I asked.

'We'll have to be off in a minute,' he said.

They were gone a long time.

'Perhaps they'll keep them there,' my mother said.

'There are a terrific lot of people to be examined,' I reminded her.

'I only hope that stuff in the bottle's been some use,' said Lottie.

A few hours later they came home. Dave looked even rottener than when he went away, but both he and my father were jubilant, because they had both been rejected.

'What did the doctor say?' Lottie wanted to know.

'He didn't say much,' Dave replied, 'but he found I wasn't fit for a labour camp.' He went and lay down on the divan. His hair was dishevelled and there were dark rings round his eyes.

I had seen him lying like that once before, a few years back. He was studying in Rotterdam, and when Father unexpectedly called on him there, it appeared that he had been on the booze for more than a week and had been drunk the whole time. Father brought him home with him. 'All that drinking,' he said, 'ruins your health.'

Dave's arm slipped off the divan and dangled limply. He had unbuttoned his shirt.

'Just a few drops out of a bottle,' he said.

The Photos

WITHIN a few days Dave had recovered from the ill effects of the brown 'medicine'. Lottie constantly ran with titbits from the kitchen to the bedroom, and my mother kept coming out with all kinds of advice.

'Give him a lot of milk, that's always very good in these cases,' she said, as if she had had to do with such things before.

'Just let him rest,' said my father. But he was soon downstairs again. However, he continued to look poorly for quite a while. Nevertheless, he went along with us to the photographer's, to have his picture taken like the others.

Mrs. Levy started it. 'We've all had ourselves photographed,' she said to my mother, when she dropped in for tea one afternoon. 'My husband and I together, and the children. You see, it's such a nice memento for later. You never know what may happen, and then you've got a photo of each other, at any rate.'

My mother agreed. 'We ought to do it too,' she said. 'I think it's a good idea.'

'Well, let's all go to Smelting, then,' Father suggested, after Mother had talked to him about it. And to us he said: 'Make sure you're presentable.'

'I'm not very photogenic,' I said. I didn't feel at all keen.

'What's that got to do with it?' said my mother.

'Besides,' I said, 'we've got enough photos, anyway. An album full of them.'

'They're nearly all just snaps,' said my mother. 'Holiday snaps taken years ago.'

'I don't care, they're nice,' I said. 'What's the good of such a best-bib-and-tucker photograph?'

'Smelting makes very good portraits,' said my mother.

I did not intend to let myself be photographed, but I went along with the others just the same. Lottie was wearing a new summer dress. She had carefully combed and put up her blue-black hair. She and Dave posed together on Mr. Smelting's rustic seat.

'Look at my hand, will you, please,' said the photographer.

He put his hand up in the air, and my brother and his wife looked at it.

'Now laugh,' he said. They both smiled simultaneously.

'Thank you,' said Mr. Smelting. 'Next, please.'

My parents also looked at his hand. 'Don't be afraid of laughing as much as you can,' he said. 'A photograph ought to show you looking as happy as possible.'

'I think I'll come back another day,' I said.

A busy time began for Mr. Smelting. The news went from one person to another. Friends dropped in to visit us regularly, and brought out their portraits. They all looked exactly alike on them. Everyone had looked at that hand and smiled.

One afternoon my mother went to call on Mrs. Levy; she wanted to show her the photos of *our* family. But in less than half an hour she was back, looking distressed.

'They've vanished,' she said. 'The whole Levy family has gone underground. The neighbours told me. They've left everything behind. I walked past the house. It looked just as if they were still living in it.'

This was the first time we had heard of anyone's going into hiding—'going underground' as it came to be called.

'Where can they have gone to?' I asked.

'Somewhere in the country, on a farm, I suppose,' said my mother. 'She didn't tell me anything about it.'

'Of course she didn't,' said my father. 'You don't go around advertising such things.'

'A pretty business,' said my mother, 'going away and leaving all your things behind, just like that.'

'When you go on holiday you leave all your things behind like that too,' I said.

'*Then* you know when you're coming back,' said my

mother. 'And with four children, as well,' she added. 'Think of all the clothes and what-not you have to take with you for that!'

'Going underground,' I said to Father, '—it seems to me like what you might call withdrawing from life.'

'Maybe they're right,' said Father. 'What can one say?'

'I should so much have liked to show them the photos,' said my mother. 'Who knows how long they'll be gone?'

It happened

---

*'Servants have ruled over us; there is none
that doth deliver us out of their hand.'*

I HAD always thought that nothing would happen to us.
And so at first I could not believe it was true. When the
telegram came from Amsterdam that morning my first
thought was: someone must have made a mistake.

But it was not so.

In order to find out the details I went with my father
to telephone at the house of a man we knew who was
married to a midwife. She was not Jewish, and con-
sequently she was allowed to keep the telephone for her
work.

The telephone was in a dark back room, where she
was busy packing an attaché case while my father tried
to get through to Amsterdam. I could not make much
of the conversation. He gave brief answers at long
intervals, as if the person at the other end of the line was
telling a long, circumstantial story. In the meantime the
midwife walked up and down the room, looked for something in a cupboard, went to another room and came
back again. She was tall and blonde. She was wearing
flat-heeled shoes, and the leather soles creaked continually.

'They started the razzia at Merwedeplein,'[1] said my father, when the call was finished. He remained standing for a moment holding the receiver in his hand.

'I'll go along with you for a short way,' said the midwife. She shut the attaché case, put on her coat, and went before us into the hall. 'These are dreadful times,' she said. 'And I'm rushed off my feet; it's almost impossible to cope.'

'They drove up in trucks in front of the house at nine o'clock last night,' my father said. He stood irresolutely in the doorway, as if he was uncertain whether to choose the street or the room where the telephone stood.

'Is it your other daughter?' the midwife asked.

He nodded. The midwife closed the front door. 'How much do I owe you?' asked my father.

'Sixty cents,' she said. 'It's nearly always daughters. People always think it's going to be a son, but in most cases it's a daughter.' She said good-bye and rode hurriedly off on her bicycle.

Slowly I walked away in the other direction with my father. He looked fixedly in front of him.

I saw the scene before my eyes. I saw the big closed trucks, and I saw my sister sitting in one of them.

'You can't do a thing,' said my father. 'You can't lift a finger to help.'

I didn't know what to say. I felt just as I had felt on that occasion, long ago, when I saw Betty almost drown. We were staying in the country with my grandparents, and had gone to the little River Dinkel for the day. I

[1] plein = square.

was seven and Betty eight. We were allowed to paddle, while my parents sat under a tree in the shade. We picked flowers at the water's edge, and Betty said: 'There are lovely ones on the other side.' She stepped towards them and I saw her disappear in the water. Speechless and motionless I stood looking at her arm, which only remained visible because she had seized hold of a tussock of grass. My father leapt fully dressed into the river and just managed to grasp her hand.

For a long time afterwards I continued to see that arm sticking out above the water. It became, for me, quite a different arm from the one she had in reality. When we played together, or when we sat at table, I looked at her arm, and could discover no resemblance between it and that other one.

We reached home. My father went inside. I stayed in the front garden, and sat down on the seat. Daffodils and tulips were blooming in the flower beds. The day before, I had gathered some of them; I could see where I had cut off the stems. Inside, my father was telling Mother about the truck that had driven up in front of the house where Betty had been living.

It would have been no use her putting her arm out of that truck. If she had done, it would have been because there was no room for the arm inside; for there was nobody who could have lifted a finger, stretched out a hand, to help her from outside.

Camping Beakers

THEY told us: 'You should have got away long ago.'
But we shrugged our shoulders. And stayed.

I was well enough now to be allowed to walk a lot,
and behind our house I had discovered a little country
road that led to a wood. It was very quiet there. Occasionally a farm labourer went past, carrying milk cans. He
glanced at the star on my coat and gave me a shy 'Good
day', but he would have said the same to anyone else.
A skinny dog walked along with me. A woman's shrill
voice called in the distance.

One day I came home from such a walk and found
three letters in the box. Three yellow envelopes. Our
names were printed on them in full, together with our
dates of birth. They were the notices we had been
expecting.

'We've got to report,' said Dave.

'I don't feel like it at all,' said Lottie. Everything in
their house was still so new.

'We shall see something of the world, anyway. It
seems—well, adventurous, to me,' said Dave.

'It'll be a terrific journey,' I said. 'I've never yet been
farther than Belgium.'

We bought rucksacks, and we lined our clothes with

fur and flannel. We stowed boxes and bottles of vitamin tablets in every pocket and corner. They had told us we had to do that. The notices also said that we had to take camping beakers with us. It was agreed that Dave should go into town and buy them.

He had almost reached the end of our road when I ran and caught him up.

'I'll go along with you,' I said. 'They won't be easy to get.'

'Do you think so?' said Dave. 'We'll see.'

We first passed a cheap bazaar, but all we saw there were earthenware beakers. 'They'd get broken too easily on the way,' said Dave.

Another shop did have camping beakers, but we found those too small. 'They won't hold anything,' he said.

Finally we came to a shop that had beakers which he considered suitable. They were red, collapsible plastic beakers, and large-sized.

'What shall we get in them, d'you think?' Dave asked me.

'You can put anything you like in them, sir,' said the shop assistant. 'Milk and coffee, served hot, or wine, or lemonade. They're of excellent quality plastic, the colour doesn't come off, and they have no taste of their own. On top of that, they're guaranteed unbreakable.'

'Right, then, we'll take three,' said Dave. 'Have you only got red ones?'

'Yes,' said the assistant, 'I've only got red ones. But they're nice and bright to go camping with. Cheerful-like.'

'You're right,' said Dave. The assistant wrapped the

beakers up in a neat little parcel; Dave took it, and we left the shop.

'It's a pity we're not allowed in anywhere,' said Dave. 'Otherwise we could have had a cup of coffee here in the town, and tried them out.'

'They've got to be washed first,' I said.

On our way home we met Mr. Zaagmeyer. 'We've been to buy beakers,' Dave told him. 'Nice, red camping beakers, one for each of us.'

'Have you three had a notice as well?' Mr. Zaagmeyer asked. 'Lord, oh Lord, my son has too. I'm on my way to try and see whether anything can be done about it.'

'Why?' asked Dave. 'There *isn't* anything to be done, is there?'

'Come along with me,' said Mr. Zaagmeyer. 'Come along; I know somebody. Perhaps he can fix up something for you people as well.'

'We've already packed,' I said.

Mr. Zaagmeyer took us to see his non-Jewish friend.

'I'll help you,' said the friend, 'provided you do exactly as I say.'

'A pity,' Dave said again, 'we're already packed, we've sewed vitamin tablets all over our clothes, and we've just been and bought camping beakers.'

'If you go, you'll never come back,' Mr. Zaagmeyer's friend said. 'Be sensible.'

'They'll come and collar us if we don't report,' I said.

'Just do as I say,' said Mr. Zaagmeyer's friend. 'I expect you to call on me at nine o'clock to-night.'

On the way home, neither of us spoke a word. At last

Dave said: 'I don't understand why people try to frighten us. What on earth can they do to us, now?'

'Yes,' I said. 'What can they do to us?'

'We could have seen something of the world,' he said, musingly.

Lottie was waiting for us in the front garden. 'What a long time you've been gone!' she said. 'The doctor's been. He doesn't want you to go away, so soon after getting better,' she said to me. 'You must be careful, he said. He's left a medical certificate behind for you.'

'That settles it,' I said. 'None of us is going.'

'Yes,' said Dave, 'we'd already bought the camping beakers, too. Look.' He unpacked them and put them on the garden fence.

'What shall we do with them?' he asked.

Sealed

WE did not need to go to Mr. Zaagmeyer's friend, because Dave got a certificate as well. There were two beds in the room now, and my brother and I walked around in pyjamas all day, so as to be able to jump into bed as soon as the bell rang. Lottie was allowed to stay to look after us. But my father and mother had to go to Amsterdam, because they were over fifty.

It was a new regulation. They were permitted to take only one suitcase of clothes with them, and before they left the case, and the room they had been living in, had to be sealed.

'Have you forgotten something?' Father asked.

'No, nothing,' my mother replied. She walked up and down the room as if she was looking for something, some last thing, to take with her. Father stood gazing out of the window.

'They were supposed to come before three o'clock,' he said. He consulted his watch. 'It's already five past.'

'Do you think that case'll have to be opened again?' asked my mother.

'Oh no,' said my father, 'they haven't got time for all that. They'll just stick a seal on it, that's all . . . oh, here they are.'

Two men in black leather coats opened the garden gate and rang the bell. Dave and I were already in bed.

Lottie went to the door. The men walked straight in without saying a word.

'Has the case got to be opened?' I heard my mother ask.

'That's what we've come for,' one of the men answered.

I had seen how carefully Mother had packed everything in. And now those men would turn it all upside down, as if something they had lost lay at the bottom of the case. It reminded me of a trip to Belgium which we had taken just before the war. On the way back my mother had got very fidgety. She asked my father every five minutes whether he thought our bags would have to be opened. At first I did not understand why she was getting so worked up. But it became clear to me later, when the customs went through the case. There were two big bottles of eau de cologne in it. Import duty had to be paid on them; so mother might as well have bought them in Holland.

When the men had gone we looked at the seals.

'It'd be the easiest thing in the world to get the seals off and put something more in the case,' I said. 'You can always stick them down again with glue.' I picked at the corner of one. Sure enough, it started to come loose easily.

'Leave it,' said my father. 'We don't need anything more. After all, we're not staying away so very long.' His optimism was so unshakeable that it was infectious. I constantly asked him what he thought of the situation, only because I knew in advance that I should hear something to reassure me. When I got frightened by the stories about what was happening to our people in Poland, he

always said: 'Things won't come to that with us.' I still do not know whether he believed it himself, or whether he only said it to put heart into us.

'Look here,' he said, 'naturally, they need young people like you for the war industries, munitions and suchlike, because the men are all in the army. The older people have to go and live in Amsterdam. They're making a ghetto again there . . . it's going to be a big parish. The Rabbi'll have his hands full!'

'Let's hope it doesn't last much longer,' said my mother. I knew she was thinking about Betty. 'I'm quite O.K.,' she had written on a card which we had received from her a few days after the razzia. 'You mustn't worry at all.' Provided it didn't go on too long, she would be able to stick it out there. 'She's so strong and healthy,' everybody said, 'she'll come through all right.'

After my parents were gone, Lottie and I stood in the hall and looked at the seal that had been stuck across the doorpost. It gave the room beyond an air of mystery. As if something was hidden in it which we were not allowed to see.

'We'll go in, just as usual,' Lottie said. With her fingernail she split the seal down through the middle, where the door opened.

We felt as if we were entering a strange room. Cautiously, as though we were afraid someone might hear us, we walked round the table, put out our hands and lightly touched a chair, a small cupboard.

'They've written everything down,' Lottie whispered. 'We can't take anything out now.'

I slid a vase a few inches along the mantelpiece. 'And it's just as if it's no longer ours, too,' I whispered back. 'Why is that?'

'Because they've been pawing everything with their hands,' Lottie said.

We went out of the room and left the torn seal as it was.

In Safe Keeping

'How you've managed to stick it out in bed for so many months is a mystery to me,' said Dave. We had worn nothing but pyjamas for weeks now, and sometimes spent all day in bed, because rumours were going around that the authorities were descending on houses to check up.

'Oh, well,' I said, 'when you have to . . .'

'Yes,' said Dave, 'then you get used to it, of course. It's the same as wearing a star and not having a wireless set.'

'Though I must say, in hospital I did have more the feeling that it was for my own good,' I added.

'I say, may I borrow your tennis racket?' a voice suddenly called from outside. The french windows were open. The head of the girl from next door was sticking up over the board fence. Laughing, she looked into our room.

'Yes, of course,' I called back.

She climbed over the fence and jumped down into the garden.

'How nice,' she said, beating a little sand from her wide-skirted, flowered summer dress.

'I don't need it,' I said. 'You're welcome to it.'

'Naturally, you people don't play tennis now, do you, eh?' she said.

'No,' said Dave. 'Not now.'

'Besides,' the girl said to me, 'the doctor wouldn't have let you play tennis yet, anyway.'

'You're right,' I said. 'Come on up to my room.'

We went upstairs. While I was looking in a cupboard for my racket, the girl nosed around among my books. 'How *sweet*!' she said.

I turned. I thought she was talking about a book, but she was standing with a little china cat in her hand.

'Take it along,' I said. 'We shan't be able to stay here much longer, anyway.'

'I'd love to,' she said. 'It'd be a pity if you left all these nice things standing here.'

'That's true,' I said. 'Look out some more things—anything that takes your fancy.'

She walked round the room, picked up a vase, a wooden bowl, a little old brass box, and a few other trifles.

'Oh!' she cried. 'What a lovely bag!' She put the things she was holding down on the table, and seized a handbag that was hanging on a chair. She turned it round and round and looked at it from all sides, opened it, and took out what was in it.

'Look,' she said. 'I'll just take everything out, shall I? It's a dream of a bag.'

'It's my sister's,' I said. 'She made it herself.'

'Was she so good at leatherwork?' the girl asked.

'She made a lot of things from leather. Very pretty things.'

'I'll keep it for you,' she said.

'Right,' I said.

'I may use it now and again, mayn't I?'

'Yes,' I said, 'by all means.'

Holding the racket, the handbag and the other things in her arms, she paused and stood looking round my room, as if there was still something she had forgotten.

'That tile . . .' she said.

I took it off the wall and laid it on top of the pile.

'I'll open the door for you,' I said.

'I ought to have brought a sack with me,' she laughed.

'But, of course, you didn't know you'd have so much to carry. After all, you only came for the racket, didn't you?'

'Quite,' she said. 'It's nice that I can use yours. It's a good racket, isn't it? I thought, I'll just ask—there's no harm in asking. It's a shame to leave it lying in a cupboard, and you people won't be thinking of playing tennis yet awhile, will you now?'

I went down the stairs with her, and held the front door open for her. 'Can you manage?' I asked.

'Oh, yes.' She lingered hesitantly on the mat.

'Would you mind looking outside for me?' she asked. 'One has to be so careful these days . . . if they should see me coming out of your house like this . . . you never know . . . there's no point in asking for trouble.'

I threw my coat on over my pyjamas and looked up and down the road.

'I don't see anyone,' I said.

'Bye-bye, then.' The girl skipped out through the gate and ran into the garden of the house next door. The bag swung to and fro on her arm. The tail of the china cat stuck out of it.

Homecoming

'Know what I'm going to do?' I said to my brother one afternoon. 'I'm going to Amsterdam.'

'What on earth's come over you?' said his wife. 'I don't think that's very sensible.'

'I've had enough,' I said. 'I want to know what it feels like to wear clothes again.'

'I can understand that,' said Dave. 'And maybe you'd be better off in Amsterdam than anywhere else. We ought to go there too.'

'But how will you manage it?' asked Lottie.

'I'll take the star off my coat and get on the train. Nothing's simpler.'

'Let's hope there's no strict watch being kept, then,' said Dave.

'I'll be careful,' I said. 'I'm going, in any case.'

I wanted to visit my parents. In their letters they said they had been lucky. They had found furnished rooms in Sarphatistraat, in a big house with a garden. 'We've already met several people we know,' Father had written. 'We all live in the same district here.' Although I gathered from the letters that they were getting along quite cheerfully, I realized that they would find things pleasanter if they had one of their children with them. Especially since they were becoming more and more worried about Betty, from whom they had heard nothing further.

As soon as it was dark I would set out, I thought. I was as excited as a child going a journey for the first time. Not because I was on the point of seeing my father and mother again, but because for a brief while I would be able to act as if everything was normal.

However, at every corner on the way to the station I thought that a policeman was standing there to check up. And in the dimly-lit booking hall I felt that everyone was looking searchingly at me.

In the train I sat huddled in a corner, beside a woman who was rocking a child to sleep in her lap. Opposite me a man was smoking a pipe and staring out through the window. There was nothing to be seen. We were travelling through a dark landscape, and I forgot my fear. I began to enjoy it. I could not help humming to the monotonous rhythm of the wheels. I remembered how Betty and I often spent our holidays in Amsterdam, when we were children. Then we used to pass the time in the train by seeing which of us could think up the nicest things to fit the rhythm of the wheels. 'To *Am*-ster-dam-and-*Rott*-er-dam-with-*bread*-and-ham-and-*gin*-ger-bread!' we would chant, sometimes for mile after mile.

Amsterdam was dark and wet. There were still quite a lot of people about. They moved like wraiths along the broad pavement of the Damrak, which leads into the heart of the city from the Central Station. No one followed me.

Once arrived in Sarphatistraat I had some trouble in finding the house. Under the trees it was almost pitch dark. I went up the steps into the porches, and tried to make out the numbers of the flats opening on to the porch.

At last I found the house. It was a fair distance down the street. With my hand on the knob of the bell, ready to pull it, I remembered that I couldn't just simply ring. Things were no longer as they had been. All the people in the house would jump out of their skins.

I stood and whistled for a while, but no one seemed to hear me. So there was nothing for it but to ring all the same. I did it discreetly, and three times, one after the other. As soon as I heard someone approaching in the hall I called my name through the letter-box.

'What, is it you?' said my father, in amazement. He opened the door a little way and I slipped in.

'I thought I'd come and take a look at you,' I said gaily.

'Child, child,' said my mother, 'how did you have the courage?'

'Oh, there was nothing to it,' I said.

After the other occupants of the house had heard that there was nothing seriously the matter, they all came to look at me.

'Have you been sitting in the train—just like that?' asked one.

'Did nobody want to see your identity card?' asked another.

'Did you really dare to buy a ticket at the ticket office?'

They looked at the place on my coat where the star had been as if it was one of the sights of Amsterdam.

'There are yellow threads still on it,' somebody said.

'You'd better put it back on again now,' my mother said.

'Was the train crowded?' my father asked.

They questioned me as if I had been on a long journey —as if I came from abroad.

'You must be hungry,' said Mother. She left the room, and came back with some slices of bread and butter.

I was not in the least hungry. However, in order not to disappoint my mother I started to eat.

They all remained standing round the table, watching with faces full of such happy content that I ate every piece of bread and butter on the plate, albeit with the greatest difficulty.

In the Basement

THE house in Sarphatistraat had something sombre about it. The rooms were high, lined with dark wallpaper, furnished with heavy, solid furniture.

A week after my parents had moved in, the Jewish family to whom the place belonged suddenly vanished. That morning my father and mother sat waiting for them at the breakfast table in vain. At first they thought the people had overslept; but when none of them put in an appearance they were forced to assume that they had deemed it wiser to leave the unquiet city.

Father and Mother came to an agreement with the family upstairs (who had not been living there long either) that they should take over the whole of the ground floor. By the time I arrived to join them, Mother had settled in completely, and had arranged the rooms as she wanted them, so that the atmosphere in the house was something like that of our home in Breda. Nevertheless, with its narrow corridors, dark stairs and brown-painted doors, it remained a typical Amsterdam house. A steep spiral stair led down into a basement full of furniture, lampshades, rolls of silk and boxes of beads and dress trimmings.

After I discovered that, I spent hours there, ferreting among the musty-smelling pieces of cloth, the ribbons embroidered with gold thread, and the cold skeletons of the lampshades. As a child I had often sat rummaging in a chest full of carnival costumes which we had in the attic. I tried them all on, one after the other, and went around in them for entire afternoons. And in just the same way, I used to hang strings of beads round my neck in that basement, and walk about in those stuffy underground rooms.

One morning my father came down the stairs. He had his overcoat on and was carrying my coat over his arm.

'Put this on,' he said, 'and quickly.' My mother came down behind him.

Hastily I threw off the beads. Father switched the light out. In the half-darkness we went and sat near the grated window on the side of the house next the street. From where we sat we could see only the feet of the passers-by.

At first, nobody passed. But after a few minutes we saw big, black boots appear, jackboots, which made a loud clicking noise as they walked. They came from the house to the right of us, and they went obliquely past our window to the edge of the pavement, where a car or a truck was standing.

We also saw ordinary shoes, walking along beside the boots. Men's brown shoes, a pair of pumps worn over at the heels, and sports shoes. Two pairs of black boots stepped to the vehicle slowly, as if they had something heavy to carry.

'There are a lot of people living in the house next door,' Father whispered. 'It's a convalescent home, and there are quite a few sick folk among them.'

A couple of beige-coloured child's boots stopped in front of our window. The toes were turned slightly inwards, and the lace of one little boot was slightly darker than the lace of the other.

'That's little Lizzie,' said my mother softly. 'She grows so fast. Those boots are much too small for her already.' The child raised one foot, and the other boot jumped to and fro in front of our window as if she was playing hopscotch. Until a pair of black boots came up.

We heard the door of the house on the right slam shut. The black boots did not move. They were well-polished, had straight heels, and remained standing motionless right in front of us. We looked through our window as if it was a shop front behind which something special was exhibited for sale. My mother held her head cocked slightly to one side, because an upright bar blocked the view for her. Father looked straight before him.

The boots started to move, and we watched first the left one moving off, then the right one, then the left one, then the right one, away from the window, on to the left.

At the house to the left of ours we heard the bell ring.

We stayed sitting where we were until we saw no more boots. Then we went upstairs and hung our coats on the hallstand.

Sabbath

I LOOKED down over my mother's book, over the finger with which she traced the lines to enable me to follow the prayers, down through the lattice-work of the screen to where I saw my father standing wearing his prayer shawl. I could not help thinking of the synagogue at Breda, which was much smaller and nothing like as fine. But there Father had had a roomy pew all to himself. It had been just like a coach without wheels. To get out of it, he had to open a little round door and descend a few steps. The door squeaked, and when I heard it squeak I would look downwards.

Father would go to the centre of the building. I would follow with my eyes his shining top hat and his ample prayer shawl, which floated out behind him a little as he walked. He would ascend the stairs of the *almemmor*, the dais in the middle of the synagogue from which the scrolls of the Law are read, and whither he was 'summoned' to distribute blessings. Suddenly I would hear our names, between the half-chanted Hebrew texts. The names sounded very beautiful in Hebrew. And they were longer, because Father's name was always added to them. Then my mother would also look down through the grille and smile at Father. The other women in the gallery would nod to my mother, to show that they had heard, and wait to see whether their husbands would give *them* a blessing, so that my mother would be able to nod to them in their turn. It was a custom in the Breda congregation.

But now I saw Father sitting somewhat towards the back, on a bench among other men. He was wearing an ordinary hat, and he remained where he was until the end of the service. It was a long service. Special prayers were said for the Jews in the camps. Some women wept. In front of me one woman was sitting who blew her nose repeatedly, huddled behind her prayer book. She had on a reddish-brown *bandeau*—the wig worn by our married women—which had sagged backwards a little under her hat.

My mother had laid her prayer book beside her on the seat. She was staring fixedly into space. I put my hand on her arm.

'It's very cold in Poland now,' she whispered.

'Yes, but she was able to take warm clothes with her, wasn't she?' I said softly. 'She had a rucksack lying ready.'

Mother nodded. The cantor raised his voice in another prayer and we all stood up. Down below, someone had taken a scroll from the Ark. The scroll was covered with purple velvet, and there was a silver crown on it from which little bells hung. The scroll was carried round the building. The bells tinkled. As the scroll went past them the men kissed the tip of the velvet.

After a while, the final hymn burst forth. It is a cheerful

melody, and I never ceased to be surprised by the rather exuberant way in which the congregation plunged into it. Singing, the men folded up their prayer shawls, and the women put on their coats. I saw my father carefully stowing his shawl away in the special bag intended for the purpose.

In front of the synagogue people waited for each other. They shook hands and wished each other 'Good Sabbath.' Father was already there when we came out. I remembered how I had hated having to walk home with the rest after Sabbath service, when I was a child. I was always frightened of running into children from my school.

Most of the people quickly dispersed over the square. Some went in the direction of Weesperstraat; others made for Waterlooplein. An acquaintance of my father's asked us whether we cared to walk part of the way home with him along Nieuwe Amstelstraat.

'I've sent my wife and children into the country,' he said. 'At the moment it's better for them to be there than here.'

'Why haven't you gone with them?' my mother asked.

'Oh, well,' he said, 'that's not in my line. I'll manage all right.'

'Are you on your own at home now?' Mother asked him.

'No,' he answered, 'I'm staying with my sister. She's not doing anything about it either, for the time being.'

'What could you do, actually?' asked my father.

'Well,' said his friend, 'you can shut the door behind

you and disappear. But then, what are you going to live on?'

'Exactly,' said my father. 'You've got to live. You've got to have something to live on.'

We were standing on the corner near the Amstel river.

An ice-cold wind was blowing in our faces. My father's acquaintance shook hands all round. 'I've got to go that way, to my sister's,' he said. He crossed the bridge to Amstelstraat. A small, hunched figure, with the collar of his black overcoat right up round his ears and his hand on his hat.

We walked along beside the Amstel, and came to the bridge where it is joined by the Nieuwe Herengracht canal. We crossed the bridge, under the yellow board. The board bearing in black letters the German word 'JUDENVIERTEL'.

A couple of children with woollen scarves round their necks were hanging over the parapet, throwing bread to the seagulls. The birds, skimming low over the water, nimbly caught the scraps. A Black Maria drove down the other side of the canal. A woman pushed a window up and shouted something. The children dropped the rest of the bread on the ground and ran inside.

'Let's take the shortest way home,' said my mother. We went along the canal.

'We'll be there in no time,' said my father.

'You hear of more and more people going underground,' I said.

'Yes,' said Father. 'We'll have to see about finding something for you too.'

'No,' I said. 'I'm not going alone.'

'If we were still in Breda it'd be easier,' my mother said. 'There we should have had an address in a minute. Here we know nobody.'

'There, we might perhaps have been able to move in with the neighbours, just like that,' I said.

'Oh, we could have gone anywhere we liked,' said Mother. 'We had friends everywhere.'

'Here it costs a lot of money,' said my father. 'Where am I to get it from?'

'If only we knew more people . . .' said Mother.

'Let's wait and see,' said my father. 'Perhaps it won't be necessary. And if it *isn't* necessary, there you sit, among strangers, and you're only a nuisance and a worry to them.'

We were home once more. Father put the key in the lock. I glanced involuntarily up and down the street before I went inside.

In the living room the stove was burning and the table was laid. Mother had done that before we left. Father went to wash his hands. Then he came and stood with us at the table, took the embroidered cloth from the Sabbath bread, broke the crust off it, and divided it into three pieces while praying. He dipped the bread in salt. I muttered grace, and ate the salt crust.

'That's right,' said my father, and sat down.

The Girl

ONE Friday afternoon I went to do some shopping for my mother. 'Go to Weesperstraat,' Mother said, 'you've got all the places so handy there.'

Aunt Kate was coming to dinner. Father would have to fetch her from the Jewish Old People's Home, for she couldn't go out in the streets alone any more. She was over eighty, and was the twin sister of my grandmother, who had died some years before the war, so she was really my great-aunt. She loved it when my father came and collected her and brought her home to eat with us. Then she could talk about old times, about the days when her husband was still alive.

Round about the turn of the century she had travelled abroad a lot, and she still remembered it all. After her husband died she had gone to live in the Home, since she had no children. The worst part about it for her was that she could no longer travel.

'All the same, it's quite possible I shall go on another little trip before I die,' she said, on one occasion when she was with us, 'once the war's over.'

'Aunt Kate just loves shortbread,' my mother said. 'Don't forget to bring that.'

I promised that I wouldn't forget anything. As I was putting my coat on, Mother came out into the passage.

'Make haste back,' she said, 'it gets dark early these days.'

Her words sounded just as they had done in former years, when I was allowed to play outside for a while before dinner. Only the reason why she said them had changed.

No sooner had I shut the door behind me when a fat man came up. It was just as if he had been standing waiting for me and knew I should come out at that moment. He planted himself right in front of me, preventing me from walking on.

'What's your name?' he asked.

I told him. He had a double chin and watery eyes with big bags under them. His cheeks were red-veined.

'Huh,' he said, 'd'you expect me to believe that?'

'That is my name,' I said.

'You people always have a lot of cheek,' he said. 'Where are you going?'

'Shopping,' I said. I made to walk on.

'Hey,' he said, 'you stay here.'

I glanced from side to side, at the people passing by, but nobody took any notice of us.

It looked as if we were standing talking quite normally.

'What's your name?' he asked again.

I repeated it. His upper lip curled. He had brown teeth; the front ones leaned crookedly away from each other.

'How old are you?' he asked.

I told him.

'That's correct,' he said. He stuck his hand out. 'Your identity card.'

I was surprised he had not thought of asking for that before. I fetched it out of my bag. He snatched it from my hand and scrutinized it closely.

'Hmm', he said, 'it's someone else I'm after.' He named a name I had never heard before.

'D'you know her?' he asked. 'She must be round here somewhere.'

'No,' I said, 'I don't know her.'

'You sure?' he persisted. He came a little closer. There were grey spots of ash on the lapels of his coat. His tie was crooked.

'I don't know her,' I said again, and took a step backwards.

'Oh,' he growled. He gave me my identity card back. 'Go on, run along.'

I walked off. I had reached Weesperplein before I ventured to look round. He was still standing there, in the distance. I wondered who the girl had been. I might quite possibly have seen her once; we could have passed each other in Sarphatistraat.

Weesperstraat was very busy. The little shops were full of women with their shopping baskets, getting everything in for the Sabbath. Shopgirls and shop managers in white coats, the yellow star on the breast pocket with the pencil stuck in it, bustled about behind the counters. A fat woman with a full bag made a joke and everybody laughed. Two little boys were studying a sweetshop window with close attention. They were wearing dark

blue reefer jackets; the stars had been fixed low down on them. It looked just as if they had little windmills on their pockets, whose sails might start turning in the breeze at any moment.

I soon finished my errands and hurried back home. This time I walked along the Achtergracht, beside the water, where it was quieter. A little old woman was just going into the hospital on the corner. She was being supported by two men, and was holding a white handkerchief over her mouth.

Aunt Kate should be there by now, I thought. She would be pleased to hear I had been to buy shortbread in Wecsperstraat. 'You can't get shortbread like that anywhere else in the world,' she always said. And we believed it; after all, if *she* didn't know, who did?

When I turned the corner of Roetersstraat, I saw that the fat man was no longer there. I wanted to ask my mother whether she knew that girl; but she came to meet me in the passage with a troubled face.

'Aunt Kate has gone,' she said. 'They've all been taken away.'

'All those old people?' I asked.

My mother nodded. I gave her my full shopping bag. Aunt Kate had so much wanted to travel once more, I thought, as I went into the sitting room. My father told me what he had heard from people living near the Home.

Not until hours later did I think again about the girl who was just the same age as myself, and whom I didn't know.

Lepelstraat

As I entered Lepelstraat I saw a truck approaching at the end of the street. Men wearing steel helmets and green uniforms were sitting erect behind each other on the seats. The vehicle stopped and the men jumped out. I turned round and wanted to walk back, but another truck had already driven into the street from the other end, behind me. In that one, too, the men were sitting immobile and bolt upright, rifles between their knees, like tin soldiers in a toy car. They all jumped down at the same time, on both sides, went up to the houses and pushed open the doors. Most of them were already ajar, and so they were able to go in without trouble.

One of the soldiers came up to me. He said I had to get into the truck. Nobody was sitting in it.

'I don't live here,' I said.

'Never mind about that—get in,' said the man in the green uniform.

I stood my ground. 'No,' I said again, decidedly. 'I don't live in Lepelstraat. You ask your commandant whether Jewish people living in another street have to go along as well.'

He turned and walked towards the officer in charge, who was watching his subordinates at work from a point some yards away from the truck. They exchanged a few words, in the course of which the soldier pointed towards me once or twice.

I had remained standing at the same spot, and saw a little boy come out of a doorway close by. He had a rucksack in one hand, and a piece of bread and treacle in the other. A brown smear ran down over his chin. From beyond an open door I heard heavy footsteps on the stairs.

The soldier came back and asked for my identity card. He went with it to the officer, who looked at it and gave it back to the soldier. He muttered something; his lips moved. With the identity card in the same hand that grasped the rifle, the soldier came back to me again. He walked more slowly than he had done the first time. He trod on a scrap of paper that blew across the pavement. His helmet began immediately above his eyes; it looked as if his forehead was of green steel. The little boy in the doorway had finished his bread and treacle, and was tying the rucksack on his back.

The soldier handed me the identity card and told me I could go. I walked past the truck. A few women were sitting on the benches now. An old woman was climbing awkwardly in. She was carrying a brown blanket. A man behind her pushed her up into the truck. Somewhere, someone pounded hard on a door. A window was banged shut.

In Roetersstraat I began to run fast, and did not stop running until I reached home.

'How quick you've been!' said my mother. 'Haven't you been to the butcher's?'

'No,' I said. 'It wasn't possible.'

'Why? Was he shut?'

'No. Lepelstraat was closed.'

Next morning I walked down Lepelstraat again. It was littered with paper. Doors were standing wide open everywhere. In the dark entrance to an upstairs flat a grey cat was sitting on the steps. When I stopped to look at it, the animal fled up higher and glared down at me from the top, with arched, bristling back. A child's glove was lying on one of the steps.

A few houses farther on a door hung askew, half off its hinges. The panels were splintered and the box for letters on the inside was hanging crookedly from one nail. Some papers were sticking out of it. I could not clearly see whether they were circulars or letters. From various open windows the curtains fluttered out in the wind. On one window frame a flower-pot had fallen over on its side. Through another window I saw a table still laid for a meal. A piece of bread on a plate. A knife stuck into the butter.

The kosher butcher's shop where I was to have bought meat the day before was empty. A plank had been nailed across the door, so that no one could get in. That must have been done quite early on. From outside, the shop looked nice and neat. As if the butcher had cleaned it out thoroughly first.

The roller shutter in front of the pickle merchant's little hall was down. The vinegary smell of the casks of gherkins still hung about it. From under the shutter a wet trail ran across the pavement to the gutter. It must have come from barrels that had fallen over.

Suddenly the wind began to blow. The bits of paper whirled over the asphalt, struck against the houses. Near by, a door slammed shut. No one had come out. A window clattered. No hand was raised to close it. A shutter banged to. But it was not yet night.

Before I turned the corner I saw something on a doorpost. An enamel plate with a red eye, showing that the house was under the protection of the Night Watch Service.

The door was open.

The Men

THE night the men came I ran away, through the back garden door.

It had been a mild spring day. In the afternoon we had lain in deckchairs in the garden, and in the evening I noticed that my face was already slightly sunburnt.

Mother had been ill the whole week, but she had been well enough again to lie out in the sun that afternoon. 'To-morrow I'm going to start knitting a summer jumper for you,' she promised me. Father lay smoking a cigar in silence, and left his book unopened on his lap. In the tool shed I had found a tennis racket and a ball, with which I practised a bit, against the wall. The ball constantly flew over the top, and then I had to open the garden door and go and look for it in the road. And sometimes it landed on the other side of the fence. Between our garden and the neighbours' was a narrow ditch, with a board fence on either side of it. You could just stand upright in the narrow passage without being seen.

While I was searching for my ball there, Father came to have a look.

'That'd make a nice hiding-place,' he said.

He climbed over the fence and we squatted behind a tree which belonged neither to us nor to the neighbours.

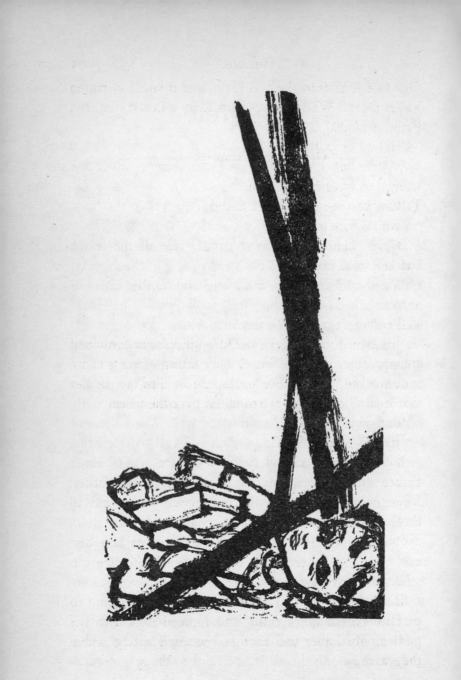

Our feet sunk into the soft earth, and it smelt of rotten leaves there. While we sat thus hidden in the dimness, Father whistled.

'Hullo,' he called.

'Where have you two got to?' asked my mother. She seemed to have been dozing.

'Can you see us?' Father asked.

'No. Where *are* you?'

'Here,' Father said, 'on the other side of the fence. Just use your eyes.'

We peered through a crack and saw Mother drawing nearer.

'I still can't see you,' she said.

'Just the job,' said Father. He straightened up and sprang agilely over the fence. 'Stay sitting where you are for a minute,' he said to me. He intimated to my mother that it was her turn to try to climb over the fence.

'But why?'

'Just try,' he replied.

Mother had to repeat the performance several times before she did it nimbly enough to please my father. Then he climbed back over the fence himself, and all three of us squatted down together in the ditch.

'No one will ever think of looking for us here,' he said. 'Let's stay here for a bit, to see whether we can stick it out for long in this position.'

But I espied my ball among the leaves. 'I'm going to practise backhand,' I cried, and jumped back into the garden. My father and mother remained sitting where they were.

'Can you see us?' Father called.

'No,' I called back. 'I can't see anything.'

They reappeared. My mother dusted herself down. 'I've got absolutely filthy in that place,' she said.

'To-morrow I'll dig out a hole, and rake the leaves away a bit, so that we can sit there in more comfort,' my father promised.

That evening, after dinner, I stood in front of the window, looking out. The street was deserted. It was so quiet that you could hear the birds chirping.

'Do come away from that window,' said Mother.

'Where's the harm in it? There's not a soul in sight,' I said. Nevertheless I turned and sat down. My mother poured out the tea. Softly she moved about between the tea trolley and us.

'Perhaps it would be better if we didn't take any tea,' said my father. 'Then we can make a quicker getaway to the garden if they should come.'

'It's so *cheerless* here without tea,' my mother objected.

Slowly the darkness came down. As Father was pulling the curtains shut the first trucks roared past.

He stood still, holding the curtain in his hand, and looked at us.

'There they go,' he said.

'They're going by,' said Mother. We listened to those sounds from outside. The roar of the trucks' engines died away. The silence lasted for some time. Then we heard more heavy vehicles pass along the street. This time it took longer for the noise to cease. But then a silence fell which we hardly dared to break. I saw my mother looking at her half-full teacup, and I knew she wanted to finish drinking her tea. But she did not move.

After a while my father said: 'We'll wait another ten minutes and then we'll put the big light on.' But before those ten minutes were up the bell rang.

It was just before nine. We remained sitting where we were, and looked at each other in surprise. As if we were asking ourselves: who could that be? As if we didn't know! As if we thought: it's just as likely to be a friend or acquaintance, dropping in for a visit! After all, it was still early in the evening, and tea had been made.

They must have had a master key.

They were standing in the room before we could stir. Two tall men, wearing light raincoats.

'Fetch our coats, will you?' Father said to me. Mother finished her cup of tea.

With my coat on, I lingered in the hall. I heard my father say something. One of the men said something in reply. I could not make out what it was. I put my ear to the door of the room. Once again I heard my father's voice, and again I could not make out what he said. Then I turned round and walked through the kitchen, into the garden. It was dark. My foot struck against something round. It must have been a ball.

I shut the garden door softly behind me and ran down the street. I did not stop running until I arrived at Frederiksplein. There was no one to be seen. Only a dog, nosing along the house fronts.

I crossed the square. It was as if I was alone in a deserted city.

Bitter Herbs

FOR the first few days I reproached myself for leaving my father and mother in the lurch. I felt that it would have been better if I had stayed with them. Without stopping to think I had run out through the garden gate, and it never entered my head to consider turning back until I stood in front of the house where my brother had gone into hiding some days before. But at that moment the church clock struck the hour after which no one was allowed to be out of doors, so I rang the bell.

'You did right,' said Dave. 'You couldn't have done anything else.'

'But they'll wonder where I've got to,' I said. 'They'll start worrying about me.'

'They'll understand,' said Dave. 'And they'll be glad you bolted.'

I thought of the Hollandsche Schouwburg, the former Jewish theatre to which all our people were taken to begin with. 'If I go and stand near the Schouwburg, and wait till they come out, perhaps they'll see me and know I'm safe,' I suggested.

But Dave said I wasn't to do it. He found it far too risky.

From neighbours in Sarphatistraat we heard that, since my flight, someone had been keeping an eye on our house the whole time. As they had my identity card they knew what I looked like, and because all my clothes were still in the house they thought I might very likely come to fetch them.

Before I ventured out into the street again I underwent a metamorphosis. Lottie bleached my hair.

I sat in front of the mirror with a sheet wrapped round me while she brushed a mixture of hydrogen peroxide and ammonia into my hair with a toothbrush. It bit into my scalp and made my eyes smart, so that I did nothing but blink, like a child that wants to keep back its tears. I tried to watch my hair changing colour in the mirror. But all I saw was the white lather of the stinging, hissing peroxide. After washing and drying, I was a redhead. But Lottie assured me that it would only take a few more such bleachings to turn my hair quite blond. I depilated my eyebrows until all that was left of them was thin, hardly visible streaks. There was no longer anything dark about my appearance. As I have blue eyes, bleached hair suited me better than it did Lottie. She had dark-brown, almost black eyes, with long, bluish-black lashes. Fair hair looked unnatural on her.

At first we thought that nothing could happen to us now. We had other identity cards, and it was just as if we were 'ordinary' people. But all the same, we did not feel safe in the street. When we saw a policeman we expected him to make straight for us, and it seemed as though every passer-by turned to look at us and knew what we were.

Finally, Mrs. K saw it too. She was the woman from

whom my brother had rented a room, under his assumed name. 'Do you people like bleached hair so much?' she asked, when she saw that mine was one colour one day and a different colour the next.

'We love it,' I said. 'And we've got such good stuff for doing it with. It's not in the least harmful.'

Perhaps Mrs. K would not have taken any further notice if Dave had not started to do it too. He emptied the entire bottle of peroxide over his head. It was not very wise of him, because it is quite impossible for a man to keep it up, and after a few weeks he would have begun to look extremely odd.

'Are you starting as well?' Mrs. K observed, with feigned friendliness.

'My husband poured my peroxide on his hair in mistake for his own lotion,' Lottie explained.

Mrs. K laughed heartily. 'I thought so,' she said.

That day she invited us to have a cup of tea with her in her sitting room. A friend of hers was coming, and it would make such a nice, pleasant evening if we were there as well. Later it appeared that her guest, a flabby fat man with cunning little eyes, had been called upon to give his verdict on us and confirm her suspicions.

When we were back in our room again, she put her head round the door. 'I think it would be better if you left early to-morrow morning,' she said. The man was putting his coat on in the hall. He went down the stairs whistling.

'I know an address in Utrecht,' said Dave. 'They'll certainly put us up there.'

'It's to be hoped they will,' said Lottie, 'for if they don't, where else can we go?'

'There are still enough doors open to us,' Dave said thoughtfully.

I could not help thinking about those doors when I lay in bed that night and could not get to sleep. I thought of the door which I always had to open on the Night of the Passover, to show the weary stranger that he was welcome and could sit down at table with us. Every year I hoped that someone would come in; but no one ever did. And I thought of the question which I, as last-born, had to ask, '*Manishtanno, halailo, haҳay*. Why is this night unlike all other nights, and why do we eat unleavened bread and bitter herbs . . .?'

Then my father would chant the story of the exodus from Egypt, and we ate of the unleavened bread and the bitter herbs, in order that we should taste again of that exodus—from year to year, for ever and ever.

Parted

———————

IT was arranged that we were to meet each other in a second-class compartment in the Utrecht train. We did go to the station together, but we bought tickets at different windows and passed through the barrier separately.

Before that, we went for a stroll along the Damrak, and Lottie suggested we should go to the cinema, just for this once. It was a very long time since we had seen a film. In the dark cinema we felt at our ease for a brief space. There, no one checked up on you. There, outward differences of face or figure were hardly detectable. In front of me a fat man was sitting, whose back prevented me from seeing part of the screen, but it didn't matter. I noticed that neither of the others paid much attention to the film either. It was, of course, a German film, and perfectly comprehensible; but not one of the three of us could have said what it was about.

When we came out it was time to catch the train. Just outside the station Dave said:

'I think it would be better if we parted now. We'll wait for each other in the second-class carriage.'

'Isn't that a very roundabout way of doing things?' I asked. 'Surely it'd be simpler to buy three tickets at once and have done with it?'

'No,' said Dave, 'it's better this way.'

'But,' I persisted, 'shouldn't we at any rate go into the hall together? Then, if anything happens, we'll be together, at least.'

'Nothing's going to happen,' said my brother. He left us and went into the booking hall. We did as he had said. I picked out a ticket window different from the ones the others used, passed through the barrier, and found the train to Utrecht.

We still had seven minutes. In the second-class carriage there was not a seat left at the window on the platform side. So I could not see Dave and Lottie coming. I had thought they would get in pretty soon after me. I had seen no signs anywhere of any special watch being kept. But they did not come.

'This *is* the train for Utrecht, isn't it?' I asked a woman sitting opposite me. I thought: perhaps I hadn't looked properly and had got into the wrong train. But the woman confirmed that it was the train to Utrecht.

'Utrecht's a nice town, don't you think?' she went on to say.

I nodded.

'It's not a patch on Amsterdam, of course,' she continued, 'but I like going there, all the same. It's got something—well, *intimate* about it, something I sometimes miss in Amsterdam.'

'Oh, yes,' I said, 'quite.' I saw a few more travellers get into the train. Dave and Lottie were not among them.

'And then,' said the woman, 'my whole family lives there, and that makes a difference, of course. Have you got relatives in Utrecht?'

'No,' I answered.

'Oh, then you've friends living there,' she said. 'So have I—very good friends, they used to live here in Amsterdam.'

A minute before the train was due to leave, my brother entered the compartment. He did not sit down and he did not look at me. He put his brief case on the seat beside me, and had got out of the train again before I could ask him any questions. The train began to move immediately, as if it had been he who had given the signal for departure.

'Is that your brief case?' the woman asked.

'Yes,' I said. 'I forgot it.'

'Nice of the gentleman to come after you with it,' she said.

We had passed the houses of East Amsterdam, and the train was now leaving the city at full speed.

'Oh,' the woman said, 'it's no distance. You're there before you know it.'

But to me the journey seemed long. I had taken the brief case on to my lap, and stared out through the window. When we approached Utrecht I got up and went into the corridor.

'Have a nice day in Utrecht!' the woman called after me.

Her words continued to echo in my ears as I crossed

the square outside the station. I could still hear them as I turned the corner into a broad shopping street and passed a cafeteria from which a greasy smell of frying billowed out.

I stopped in front of a shoe-shop window; I felt so sick I was afraid I would have to vomit. 'Take a deep breath, then it'll stay down all right,' the nurse in the hospital had always said to me, whenever I showed such tendencies during my treatment. I took several deep breaths, and that helped.

A little later I was standing before the house I was supposed to go to. It was above a grocer's, Dave had said only that morning. As soon as I rang, the door opened. I walked in and up the stairs. They were steep stairs, covered with a dark red carpet. An economy bulb glimmered on the first landing. A stair rod was loose here and there on the following flight of stairs. It was an even longer, steeper flight than the first one. At the top I could see a man and a woman standing. They looked at me and said nothing.

'I'm . . .' I began.

'We know,' the man cut in. 'Your brother rang up from the station at Amsterdam to say that only you would be coming.'

'Did he say anything else?' I asked.

'Yes,' said the man. 'His wife was stopped at the barrier. He was going to join her as soon as he had finished telephoning.'

I followed them in. They motioned to me to sit down in a deep, comfortable chair.

'I'm very sorry,' the man said, 'but I've no room here. I know a good address for you, though.'

The woman set a cup of tea down in front of me. I was still clutching the brief case. I put it across my knees and drank.

The Crossroad

I WENT back to Amsterdam the same evening. 'You're welcome to stay the night here,' they said at Utrecht; but I didn't want to. I wanted to go back at once. They begged me at any rate to eat something, or, at least, lie down for a while and rest. But I wasn't tired, and I had no desire to eat.

Before leaving, I telephoned an acquaintance in Amsterdam. 'Just come along here,' said Jan. He was a non-Jewish boy I had met some weeks before, when I called on a Jewish family. It was after my parents had gone. 'If you're in trouble, ring me up,' he had said. I hadn't given him another thought.

Some hours later, carrying my brother's brief case, I stepped into the train. I didn't bother to note whether passes or people were being scrutinized; I didn't look out for police or soldiers; I didn't take the trouble to choose any particular carriage. A great load of fear had fallen off my shoulders. I felt that if I were to be captured now, at any rate I should no longer have that feeling of having been left behind alone.

Jan was waiting for me at Amstel Station.

'I've had a word with Uncle Hannes,' he said. 'He's coming to fetch you to-morrow.'

I didn't ask who Uncle Hannes was. It sounded as if

Jan was talking about an uncle of mine, and I left it at that.

'Is that brief case all you've got?' Jan asked.

'I've got a suitcase with some clothes in it,' I answered. 'It's still at Mrs. K's.'

Jan said he would collect the suitcase for me.

Next day I met Uncle Hannes at the bus stop in Surinameplein. He was an old man with a red, weather-beaten face covered with tiny wrinkles. I had the suitcase of clothes with me. Dave's brief case I had left behind with Jan.

I didn't know where we were going, and I didn't ask. I saw that the bus was leaving the city behind, and finally we came out on a country road running between meadows.

At a crossroad Uncle Hannes motioned to me, and we alighted. The bus drove swiftly off. The old man brought a bicycle out from behind a tree, and tied my case on to the carrier.

'Just walk straight down this road,' he said, 'until you come to the fifth farm.' He nodded to me, and got on the bike.

I stood at the crossroad and watched Uncle Hannes cycle off; the case swung to and fro behind him. A cloud of dust hung in the distance, hiding the bus from view. It must have been about midday, for the sun was high in the heavens. Above the fields the air throbbed with the heat.

I trod in the tracks left by Uncle Hannes' bicycle, and felt the sun burning on my head and back. I was glad the old man had taken my suitcase, because the walk to the fifth farm turned out to be a long one.

When I got there, I saw an old farm-woman standing in the yard.

'Come in,' she said.

In a low-ceilinged, dark room, a lot of people were sitting round a long table. Uncle Hannes sat at the head of it. Someone pushed a chair up for me, and put a beaker of milk down in front of me. The milk was cool. In the middle of the table stood a big plate of open sandwiches. Everyone helped himself or herself. The woman next to me put a couple of sandwiches on my plate.

'You've got to eat, child,' she said, smiling. She had dark hair, which she wore in a heavy bun at the back of her neck. Her hands were long and slender; beautiful hands, with slim fingers and pointed nails. The hands of a woman who had been accustomed, on Friday night, to spreading the white damask cloth over the table; who put ready, beside the bottle of wine, the sacred silver cup from which all the members of the family would drink to usher in the Sabbath; and who covered the Sabbath bread with its embroidered napkin. I thought of my mother—how she would lay the table for the Friday night feast, and how we waited in the brightly lit, familiar room for my father to come home from the synagogue. Then we would inaugurate the Sabbath with a mouthful of wine and a piece of the bread.

'Do eat something,' said the woman next to me. I took a piece of bread and meat and looked down the table. Women wearing brightly coloured aprons were sitting at it. Like the men, who wore overalls, they were all dark-complexioned. A small boy opposite looked curiously at me with dark-brown eyes, while he chewed his sandwich with bulging cheeks.

The woman next to me filled my beaker with milk again.

'My daughter's the same age as you,' she said. She smiled.

'Oh yes?' I said. 'It was very hot on the road.'

'It's nice and cool here,' she said. 'I don't know where she is.'

'Who?' I asked.

'My daughter,' she replied.

'Oh yes,' I said. And then: 'I had an awfully long walk.'

'This is a very out-of-the-way place,' the woman said. 'She should have been here too; it could easily have been managed.'

'Yes,' I said, 'it's an awfully long way from the crossroad.'

'Are you staying here?' she asked.

'I don't know,' I said.

After the meal Uncle Hannes folded his hands and prayed. The others bowed their heads, and when the grace was finished they stood up and left the room. I remained sitting alone at the table.

'You've seen how many I'm hiding here?' Uncle Hannes said to me.

I nodded. 'Yes,' I said, 'I've seen.'

'I've no room left for you,' he said. 'You'll have to move on.'

'Very well,' I said.

'The boy'll take you,' Uncle Hannes continued. He went over to the window. A red-cheeked girl came in and cleared the table.

'D'you see that tree there?' he asked, pointing outside. I rose from the empty table and went and stood beside him. 'When you get to that tree you'll see a railway crossing. Wait for the boy there.'

The red-cheeked girl started to sweep the floor. Straws and bread crumbs lay on the ground. A few crusts lay under the chair where the boy with the dark eyes had been sitting. I walked hesitantly to the door, not knowing whether I had to leave at once or not. Uncle Hannes was still staring out through the window. The girl was brushing the crumbs into a dustpan.

'All the best,' said Uncle Hannes. He turned and nodded to me.

I left the room. My suitcase was standing in the passage. Beyond the open door were the hot sun and the heavy smell of manure. I crossed the farmyard and walked up the road, without looking round.

The Bed

THE boy came riding towards me on one bicycle and pushing another. I was standing waiting for him at the open, unguarded level crossing, and saw his forelock of very fair hair flapping above a face burnt red by the sun. He put the bicycles against a post, took my case and tied it on to the carrier of his own cycle.

'We've got to go that way,' he said, and pointed to a path running across a meadow. I nodded and got on to the other cycle.

He rode in front of me along the sandy track. It had become even hotter. A horse was standing looking over a fence, and switched his tail to chase the flies away. Here and there a few cows were grazing; languidly they turned their heads and stared after us.

The boy cycled on without looking round. The path became more and more difficult to ride on because of the dry, loose sand. I had to pedal hard in order not to slip. But when we had turned into another track, the going was better. We came out on to a canal, with cottages on both sides of it. The boy slackened his pace to allow me to ride beside him, and said: 'We're nearly there.' He had tied his handkerchief round his neck.

Everywhere women were busy scrubbing the cobbles in front of their houses and cleaning the windows with

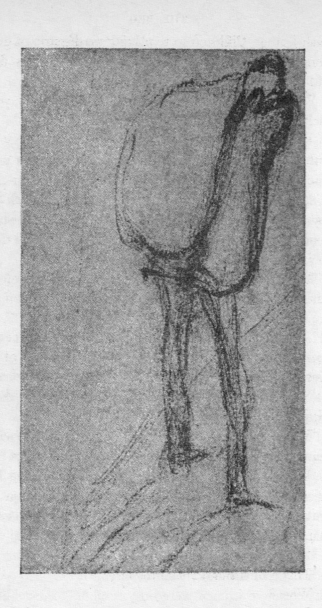

wash-leather. Children were playing on the strip of grass along the water. A fisherman sat gazing at his float without moving.

We got off at one of the houses. My clothes were sticking to my body.

'Here it is,' said the boy. We walked along a gravel path leading round behind the house, to where a door stood open giving access to the kitchen.

A woman was sitting at a table peeling potatoes. She had a thin face with a sharp, lean nose, and fair hair which hung in untidy wisps.

'Here she is,' said the boy.

'Who?' the woman asked, looking up from her potatoes.

'The girl,' he answered.

'What, already?' The woman sat with a half-peeled potato in her hand, and brushed a wisp of hair out of her eyes with the other hand.

'You knew about it, didn't you?' said the boy. 'After all, you said you could.'

'Yes, so I did,' said the woman. She spoke in a drawling voice. 'But I didn't know she'd be coming so soon.'

'Well, she's come,' said the boy. I was standing half in and half out of the doorway, with one foot on the gravel and the other on the doorstep. The woman glanced at me and went on peeling her potatoes.

'We haven't got a bed for her,' she said.

'That'll be brought,' said the boy.

'When?'

'Perhaps to-day, but more likely to-morrow, I think,'

'If we could only bank on that.'

'I'm off,' the boy said. He walked out and raised his hand. 'All the best,' he said to me.

He rode away, just as I had seen him approaching at the level crossing, pushing one cycle along beside him.

'Take a seat,' the woman said.

I sat down on the other side of the table. The potatoes fell with a splash into the zinc tub. The water spattered

against my leg, and every time it did I shivered. But I did not move my leg away. With each peeled potato I waited for the drops of water, like a person dangerously athirst who is given something to drink in sips.

'We eat a lot of potatoes,' the woman said, when the tub was full.

'You must have a big family,' I said.

'There are six of us,' she answered, 'and another on the way.'

'There were five of *us*,' I said. I could not remember so many potatoes being peeled in our home.

'Have the others all gone?' she asked.

'Yes.'

'Not one ever comes back from there, they say.' She looked up. Outside, there had been a sound of feet crunching the gravel. A couple of boys ran into the kitchen. A man followed them. A big, stoutly-built man with enormous hands. He looked at me in silence. The boys had also stopped short when they saw me.

'We haven't got the bed yet,' the woman said.

'Oh?' said the man. 'Aren't they bringing it, then?'

'The boy said perhaps it would come to-day, but if not, to-morrow.'

'Oh, well,' he said, 'she can sleep with you for the time being, and I'll crawl in with the boys.' He sank into an old armchair and put his feet up on the edge of the table. He was wearing thick black socks. He had left his clogs standing outside the door.

'We'll simply say you're our niece from Rotterdam,' he said to me.

'We haven't any relations in Rotterdam,' the woman objected.

'We *have* relations in Rotterdam,' he said. 'Anyway, I've a cousin who used to live there.'

'And suppose they don't bring the bed?' the woman began again.

'Then I'll go and fetch it,' said the man. He rolled a cigarette. The woman threw wood into the stove, and put the pan of potatoes on it. The wood crackled, and gave out a smell of resin and smoke. The children had gone out again. Occasionally they peeped in through the window. It grew stiflingly hot in the kitchen.

The woman put some plates out on the table.

Seven plates, I counted.

The Top

ON the shore of the lake Rinus, our neighbour, was sitting fishing. I went and sat down beside him, and looked at his float.

'Want to go rowing?' he asked. He sat there motionless, with his fishing rod in his hand. His wooden leg stuck out before him in the grass, like an oar someone had left lying there.

'Yes,' I said, 'I'd like to do a bit of rowing this afternoon.'

'Right you are,' he said, 'you take the boat. I shan't be needing her.'

I had been allowed to borrow his rowing-boat several times before, for he did not use it so often himself. He usually sat fishing on the bank. He had ceased to do very much since he had lost his leg—in an accident with a tractor, he had told me.

I remained sitting where I was for a while. The sun was warm to my back; it made me so drowsy I felt I should have liked nothing better than stay lying beside the water the whole afternoon. But I had to go to the village.

'Look,' said Rinus, 'there's another of 'em.'

At first I thought he had caught something; but he was looking up into the blue sky, where a moving silver spot was droning forward.

'It won't last much longer,' he said. 'You see.' I thought of my father, who had always said that too.

Rinus's eyes returned to his float. Even when more aircraft flew over, he still continued to look at the water. I got up and went to the boat, pushed off, and rowed with slow strokes to the middle of the shallow lake.

I saw Rinus getting steadily smaller. The lapping of the water against the side of the boat was the only sound I heard.

Without realizing where I was going, I found myself among the reeds.

I pulled the oars into the boat and sat still. Everything looked now as if life was normal. I was out on the water rowing, on a summer afternoon. A train whistled in the distance. There were people sitting in it who were going on holiday. Over the tops of the reeds I could see the glasshouses of the Aalsmeer nurseries. They were full of flowers. Flowers to put in vases. Flowers for a birthday. Many happy returns of the day, and here are a few flowers for you. I was out rowing this afternoon. It was heavenly on the water.

A frog leapt with a splash between the reeds. I had to get a move on. I manœuvred myself out from among the stems and rowed on, in the direction of the village.

I had arranged to meet Jan in the café at the station. I went in and sat down in front of the window to wait for him. There were few customers. German songs were coming from a gramophone. Outside, children were playing with a top. Behind them I saw Jan coming along with my brother's brief case under his arm.

'D'you like it all right here?' he asked, when he was sitting opposite me. He took a few books out of the case.

I nodded. 'I'd sooner be in Amsterdam, though,' I said.

'Why?' asked Jan. 'You're pretty snug here. In Amsterdam it's nothing like as safe for you.'

'It's just as if I'm on holiday,' I said. 'I go rowing a lot, I lie in the sun, I help a bit about the house, and for the rest I don't do a thing.'

'In Amsterdam you wouldn't be able to do a thing either,' he said.

'Did you make inquiries for me?' I asked.

'Yes,' he answered, looking out through the window. 'They've been sent on.'

I followed his gaze. 'It's the top season,' I said.

A little girl was spinning her top on the pavement. It was a red top; she lashed at it with her whip, and sent it flying in a graceful arc into the roadway, where it pirouetted round like a ballet dancer, right in front of a heavy truck.

Jan toyed with a beer mat. He tipped it on its rim on the table top, and made it roll off on to his waiting fingers.

Some German soldiers went by in the street. The sound of their heavy footsteps echoed long after they had passed. The little girl had found her top smashed to pieces by the truck.

'They'll come back, won't they? Don't you think so?' I asked.

'Yes,' said Jan. 'Perhaps it'll soon be over now.'

'Let's be going,' I said.

We rose to our feet. As I went out through the revolving door a German soldier came in. We turned in the door at the same time.

Outside, the child stood crying over her top.

Someone Else

THE bed which Uncle Hannes had promised to bring did not come, nor did the man go to fetch it. He always came home at night tired out, and he got up in the morning before the crack of dawn. He was a day-labourer on a farm, and the work he had to do there was very heavy, especially in the summer months. On Sundays he took things easily, and slept for most of the day. Now and again he teased and played about with his wife, but not for long, because she very soon lost her temper.

All that time I had to sleep with the woman, while the man slept in another bed with the boys. It was very stuffy up in the low attic bedroom, which was never aired. I slept badly, for I did not dare to move, frightened as I was to touch the woman. She had told me that she never took a bath. 'After all, I'm not dirty,' she said. 'I put clean clothes on every week.'

'I suppose your family had a bigger house?' the man said.

'Yes,' I replied.

'And beds enough to go round?' asked the woman.

'Oh, quite a lot,' I said. 'We often had guests.'

'How many beds did you have?' the woman wanted to know.

I fell to thinking. I could no longer picture the house clearly. I saw the street in Breda, the meadow on one side and the front gardens on the other; the hole in the road which I always cycled over, the sagging kerbstone at which I always turned to ride up across the pavement to the front door, the little window in the door, which was open and through which you could put your arm in order to pull the catch and open it from inside. I saw the inner glass door that fell back squeaking when you pushed it, the hall, the doors of the rooms. The stairs.

'I don't remember,' I said.

'Oh, well,' the woman said, 'there will have been enough of them.'

'I think so,' I said.

'It's a shame, such a nice house,' she said.

'What's a shame?' the man asked.

'Well,' said the woman, 'a house like that, with all sorts of things in it.'

'When the war's over,' I said, 'we'll go back there and live in it again, I suppose.'

'Oh yes,' said the man. He rolled a cigarette and looked at me. 'Oh yes,' he said again, after he had moistened the cigarette paper with his tongue.

It was the last evening I was to spend with them. Next day I was to go. The money which Dave had left behind for me in his brief case was running out. Since I could no longer pay, I did not want to be a burden any more to a family of poor people. Jan knew an address for me at Heemstede, near Haarlem.

I was sitting at the kitchen table bleaching my hair.

Black was showing through again everywhere. The strong preparation, which had turned me almost platinum blonde through frequent use, had long ceased to hurt at all.

'It's better when you're naturally blonde,' the woman said.

'But she isn't,' said the man. 'If she was, she wouldn't be here.'

'Your sort of people are always dark, aren't they?' she asked.

'No,' I answered, 'not always.'

'But you can always see what they are, all the same,' she said, stroking her round belly pensively. 'I knew a Jew once,' she went on. 'He was a nice man. He often visited the lady where I was in service.'

Next day I met Jan at the bus stop. I saw him glance at my hair.

'Can you see anything?' I asked.

'You've got nice and fair,' he said.

'It doesn't look unnatural, does it?'

'No,' he assured me, 'there's nothing suspicious-looking about you.'

But I was not so certain. Although I had accustomed myself perfectly to the idea that one day I too should get caught, I did not feel very comfortable travelling.

'Just behave normally,' said Jan.

I thought of the time when I really had been normal. I asked myself what that had been like. I had forgotten how I had looked about me when I walked in the street, how I had felt when I stepped into a train, what I had said when I went into a shop.

Jan had brought my new identity card with him. He gave it me before we entered the bus. I had already thrown the old one away. It had cost a lot of money, but it had been very bad. This one cost nothing.

'What name have you given me?' I asked.

'A beautiful one,' he answered.

Involuntarily I thought of an aunt of mine who had once been very seriously ill. Prayers had been said for her in the synagogue—the special prayer for a very sick person. She had been given another name, a beautiful name belonging to someone in the Bible. And she had recovered.

In the bus, I looked at the identity card. At my photograph with fair hair, and my thumbprint. I read the name. It was as if I was being introduced to myself. I murmured it under my breath a few times. I had become someone else.

Later, when we were walking beside a narrow canal in Heemstede, Jan pointed to a low, old house.

'Look,' he said, 'here it is. You'll be perfectly safe here.'

We went over a bridge with an iron gate in front of it. A tall, fair-haired girl in an overall came to meet us.

I told her my name—my new name.

EPILOGUE

The Tram Stop

SOME weeks after the Liberation I visited my uncle at
Zeist. The Germans had left him alone because he was
married to a Gentile woman. Although I had not written
to him beforehand, he was standing at the tram stop.

'How did you know I was coming?' I asked him.

'I wait at the stop every day,' he said. 'I look to see
whether your father's coming.'

'But you've had the news from the Red Cross too,
haven't you?'

'Yes,' he said. 'They can say all that; but I don't believe
it. You never can tell, can you?'

We crossed the little square and walked to his house,
which lay a minute or two away from the tram stop. I
had not seen my uncle for years. I found him greatly
changed. He could not have been much more than fifty,
but he walked beside me with weary, slouching steps like
a man who has nothing more to expect from life. His
hair had gone as white as snow, and his face was yellow
and sunken. Although he had always looked very like
my father, I could no longer trace the slightest resemblance between them. There was nothing left of the gay
and carefree uncle of former days.

He paused before the door of his house.

'Don't say anything about it to your aunt,' he said, stooping down towards me. 'She doesn't understand, anyway.'

He put the key into the lock. I walked up the stairs behind him. In a small, dark room my aunt was standing pouring out tea. My uncle sat down in an armchair by the window.

'You can see the tram coming from here,' he said. 'That's very convenient. There's a regular service again now between Zeist and Utrecht.' He got up and slouched out of the room.

'Uncle is ill,' his wife said to me. 'He doesn't know it himself, fortunately, but there's no possibility of his getting better. He took it terribly to heart, what happened to the family.' I nodded. I said that you could see it by looking at him, and that I found him so much altered.

'Sssh,' she said, putting her finger to her lips. He came back in again.

'Look,' said my uncle, showing me one or two dark-coloured items of clothing which he was carrying over his arm. 'This is a very nice suit, and it's in perfect condition.'

'Is it yours?' I asked.

'I've kept it all these years,' he said. 'It's been hanging nice and tidy in the wardrobe, with plenty of mothballs.' There was a hint of triumph in his voice as he whispered, 'for your father.'

He hung the suit carefully over a chair, and went on: 'I've got a pair of shoes standing in the cupboard, too. Good as new, they are. Would you like to see them?'

'Presently,' I said. But he forgot about them; for when I rose to go after a while, he quickly threw on his coat.

'I'll walk along with you,' he said, looking at his watch. 'The tram'll be here any minute.'

But the tram was already there and on the point of leaving. I said good-bye in a hurry and jumped in.

As we drove off, I waved to him from the rear balcony. But he did not wave back. He was looking at the tram approaching in the other direction, from Utrecht, and I realized that he had meant that one. Before we turned the corner I saw him, a small, bowed figure, scrutinizing the travellers who got out at the stop.

After that I went to see him several more times. I never sent word beforehand to say I was coming. He was always standing at the tram stop. Each time he looked older and more ill, and each time he showed me the suit he was keeping in his wardrobe.

One day I heard from my aunt that he was dead. I went again to Zeist, and, sitting in the tram, I thought how strange it would be not to see my uncle at the stop. Involuntarily I looked about me as I stepped out.

In the same half-dark room my aunt was sitting at the table doing a crossword puzzle. In her hand she held a pencil with a well-sharpened point. I went and sat down in the chair beside the window, and pushed the curtain a little to one side. At the end of the road I could see part of the shelter at the tram stop.

'He liked to sit there so much,' my aunt said. 'He looked out for the tram.'

'You can see it coming from here,' I said.

'Yes,' she replied, 'that's what he always said. I must say, I've never really been able to see it properly.' She came and stood behind me and bent over me. 'It's hardly possible,' she said. 'You can scarcely see anything of it.'

But that was not true. From my uncle's chair, the stop was clearly visible. And now I also understood why Uncle had said that it was best not to talk about it to my aunt.

Just before I left, she came in carrying the suit.

'Look,' she said. 'Uncle said I was to give this to you.'

'I can't do anything with it,' I said. 'Give it to someone who can use it.'

She was bending over her crossword again as I left the room. I walked slowly to the stop. I had already seen that no tram was waiting there yet to take me back. But in the meantime one had arrived from the other direction.

I stood looking at the people who got out, as if I was waiting for someone. Someone with a familiar face, that would suddenly appear right in front of mine. But I lacked my uncle's faith. They would never come back— not my father, not my mother, nor Betty, nor Dave or Lottie.

FOR THE BEST IN PAPERBACKS, LOOK FOR THE 🐧

In every corner of the world, on every subject under the sun, Penguin represents quality and variety – the very best in publishing today.

For complete information about books available from Penguin – including Puffins, Penguin Classics and Arkana – and how to order them, write to us at the appropriate address below. Please note that for copyright reasons the selection of books varies from country to country.

In the United Kingdom: Please write to *Dept E.P., Penguin Books Ltd, Harmondsworth, Middlesex, UB7 0DA.*

If you have any difficulty in obtaining a title, please send your order with the correct money, plus ten per cent for postage and packaging, to *PO Box No 11, West Drayton, Middlesex*

In the United States: Please write to *Dept BA, Penguin, 299 Murray Hill Parkway, East Rutherford, New Jersey 07073*

In Canada: Please write to *Penguin Books Canada Ltd, 2801 John Street, Markham, Ontario L3R 1B4*

In Australia: Please write to the *Marketing Department, Penguin Books Australia Ltd, P.O. Box 257, Ringwood, Victoria 3134*

In New Zealand: Please write to the *Marketing Department, Penguin Books (NZ) Ltd, Private Bag, Takapuna, Auckland 9*

In India: Please write to *Penguin Overseas Ltd, 706 Eros Apartments, 56 Nehru Place, New Delhi, 110019*

In the Netherlands: Please write to *Penguin Books Netherlands B.V., Postbus 195, NL–1380AD Weesp*

In West Germany: Please write to *Penguin Books Ltd, Friedrichstrasse 10–12, D–6000 Frankfurt/Main 1*

In Spain: Please write to *Alhambra Longman S.A., Fernandez de la Hoz 9, E–28010 Madrid*

In Italy: Please write to *Penguin Italia s.r.l., Via Como 4, I-20096 Pioltello (Milano)*

In France: Please write to *Penguin Books Ltd, 39 Rue de Montmorency, F-75003 Paris*

In Japan: Please write to *Longman Penguin Japan Co Ltd, Yamaguchi Building, 2–12–9 Kanda Jimbocho, Chiyoda-Ku, Tokyo 101*

A CHOICE OF PENGUINS

Better Together Christian Partnership in a Hurt City
David Sheppard and Derek Warlock

The Anglican and Roman Catholic Bishops of Liverpool tell the uplifting and heartening story of their alliance in the fight for their city – an alliance that has again and again reached out to heal a community torn by sectarian loyalties and bitter deprivation.

Fantastic Invasion Patrick Marnham

Explored and exploited, Africa has carried a different meaning for each wave of foreign invaders – from ivory traders to aid workers. Now, in the crisis that has followed Independence, which way should Africa turn? 'A courageous and brilliant effort' – Paul Theroux

Jean Rhys: Letters 1931–66
Edited by Francis Wyndham and Diana Melly

'Eloquent and invaluable ... her life emerges, and with it a portrait of an unexpectedly indomitable figure' – Marina Warner in the *Sunday Times*

Among the Russians Colin Thubron

One man's solitary journey by car across Russia provides an enthralling and revealing account of the habits and idiosyncrasies of a fascinating people. 'He sees things with the freshness of an innocent and the erudition of a scholar' – *Daily Telegraph*

They Went to Portugal Rose Macaulay

An exotic and entertaining account of travellers to Portugal from the pirate-crusaders, through poets, aesthetes and ambassadors, to the new wave of romantic travellers. A wonderful mixture of literature, history and adventure, by one of our most stylish and seductive writers.

The Separation Survival Handbook Helen Garlick

Separation and divorce almost inevitably entail a long journey through a morass of legal, financial, custodial and emotional problems. Stripping the experience of both jargon and guilt, marital lawyer Helen Garlick maps clearly the various routes that can be taken.

A CHOICE OF PENGUINS

The Russian Album   Michael Ignatieff

Michael Ignatieff movingly comes to terms with the meaning of his own family's memories and histories, in a book that is both an extraordinary account of the search for roots and a dramatic and poignant chronicle of four generations of a Russian family.

Beyond the Blue Horizon   Alexander Frater

The romance and excitement of the legendary Imperial Airways Eastbound Empire service – the world's longest and most adventurous scheduled air route – relived fifty years later in one of the most original travel books of the decade. 'The find of the year' – *Today*

Getting to Know the General   Graham Greene

'In August 1981 my bag was packed for my fifth visit to Panama when the news came to me over the telephone of the death of General Omar Torrijos Herrera, my friend and host...' 'Vigorous, deeply felt, at times funny, and for Greene surprisingly frank' – *Sunday Times*

The Search for the Virus   Steve Connor and Sharon Kingman

In this gripping book, two leading *New Scientist* journalists tell the remarkable story of how researchers discovered the AIDS virus and examine the links between AIDS and lifestyles. They also look at the progress being made in isolating the virus and finding a cure.

Arabian Sands   Wilfred Thesiger

'In the tradition of Burton, Doughty, Lawrence, Philby and Thomas, it is, very likely, the book about Arabia to end all books about Arabia' – *Daily Telegraph*

Adieu: A Farewell to Sartre   Simone de Beauvoir

A devastatingly frank account of the last years of Sartre's life, and his death, by the woman who for more than half a century shared that life. 'A true labour of love, there is about it a touching sadness, a mingling of the personal with the impersonal and timeless which Sartre himself would surely have liked and understood' – *Listener*